P9-CFL-007

Also by Nancy Wood

Poetry

Spirit Walker
Many Winters
War Cry on a Prayer Feather
Hollering Sun

Photography

Taos Pueblo
The Grass Roots People
Heartland New Mexico: Photographs from the Farm Security Administration, 1935–43
In This Proud Land (with Roy Stryker)

Fiction

The Man Who Gave Thunder to the Earth
The King of Liberty Bend
The Last Five Dollar Baby

Nonfiction

When Buffalo Free the Mountains
Colorado: Big Mountain Country
Clearcut: The Deforestation of America

DANCING MOONS

Poems by NANCY WOOD
Paintings by FRANK HOWELL

A Doubleday Book for Young Readers

A Doubleday Book for Young Readers
Published by
Delacorte Press
Bantam Doubleday Dell Publishing Group, Inc.
1540 Broadway
New York, New York 10036
Doubleday and the portrayal of an anchor with a dolphin are trademarks of Bantam Doubleday Dell Publishing Group, Inc.

Library of Congress Cataloging-in-Publication Data
Wood, Nancy C.
Dancing moons: poems by Nancy Wood; paintings by Frank Howell.
p. cm.
Summary: A collection of poems based on the spirituality and teachings of the Taos Indians of New Mexico.
ISBN 0-385-32169-4
1. Indians of North America—New Mexico—Poetry. 2. Taos Indians—Poetry. [1. Taos Indians—Poetry. 2. Indians of North America—Poetry. 3. American poetry.] I. Howell, Frank, ill. II. Title.
PS3573.0595D36 1995
811'.54—dc20 *94-24818*
CIP
AC

The text of this book is set in 12-point Palatino.
Book design by Trish Parcell Watts
Manufactured in the United States of America
October 1995
10 9 8 7 6 5 4 3 2 1

For Karen Wojtyla,
who cares

Two Gray Hills Woman

PREFACE

The world is hard up for simple things. I don't mean the artificial simplicity of politics, religion, or social argument. I mean things that naturally abound—exploding sunsets, rippling streams, the sighing of the wind, the chirping of crickets. Beauty. Mystery. Wonder. Essential truths that connect us, in an age of frightening greed and disregard, to the core of life itself.

I live in the southwestern part of the country. At daybreak a raven sits in the juniper tree outside my window and awakens me with a persistent call. In that voice I recognize a wild, unbroken continuity. For a moment, I see him against the searing heat of an extinct volcano that used to erupt not far from here. He endures.

On my back patio a little olive-drab lizard, looking like a miniature dinosaur, pushes himself up and down in the sunlight. In his goofy aerobics I see a reflexive motion as old as the first reptile. He offers reassurance whenever I'm afraid. He, also, endures.

The coyotes who prowl the nearby wilderness serenade me all night long. When I listen carefully, I realize they are singing many different songs. In their voices I sense the excitement of a language older than words. Those coyotes not only endure, they survive all of man's attempts to kill them with poison, bullets, or steel traps.

Simple truths are what get lost amid the anxiety of our technological world. The vacant look of teenagers milling around shopping malls bothers me. So do the harsh voices of politicians and religious leaders, telling us what we may or may not do with our lives. Spiritual bankruptcy is manifest in computers, call waiting, application forms, income tax forms, interstates, snowmobiles, fast-food chains, network TV, Wal-Mart, Disney, and all things plastic. The world is reinventing itself into conformity, trivia, and dehumanization. *Koyaanisqatsi*, the Hopi call it: turmoil, despair, life out of balance. Centuries ago, they predicted the moral and spiritual crisis that is crippling our nation today.

The Pueblo Indians of New Mexico have been my friends for more than thirty years. They taught me to examine the depths of a wild rose, to ponder the meaning of fresh leaves, sleepy turtles, river stones, and passing clouds. They took me into the mountains, where I felt a mysterious healing grace. They showed me how to lie facedown on the earth, to rediscover the cyclical nature of leaves, flowers, and grass. They taught me how to listen. How to catch the wind. How to converse with streams. How to accept the raven and the coyote as my spirit guides. How to recognize my fragile connection to all life that has gone before and all that will follow after.

Thus, when I hold an ancient Indian grinding stone in my hand, I imagine that long-ago woman, kneeling over a stone metate to grind corn or to pound wild meat until it was tender enough to roast over coals. If her life was hard, there were rewards: watching the same white clouds that I see above my head, walking the same red earth, breathing the same pure air. I feel a kinship with her when I find pottery shards scattered in the wilderness. Who was the woman who painted those simple designs on a clay pot? What did she think about when she worked? Did her children live to grow up? Was she loved?

Native Americans have lived on this continent some twenty thousand years. They based their lives on everyday experience and created a religion from it; they had no words for sin, guilt, or redemption, no concept of heaven or hell. Each individual was responsible for himself or herself; each worked for the greater good of the tribe. Their actions were justified by an intricate system of beliefs unacceptable to European invaders, who managed to destroy, in little more than five hundred years, nearly everything native people had held dear for millennia.

Native Americans did not invent bombs, wheels, chemicals, or concrete; they did not create environmental pollution, urban sprawl, traffic jams, or crime. In their world, the Great Spirit abided in all living things, offering harmony, meaning, and acceptance. They did not have to look far to discover a sense of purpose in their lives; as the sun rose, so did they. As trees lived and died, so did they. Each moment offered a unique lesson. When spring came, they noticed blossoms and birds. When a bear crossed their path, they invented a story. Songs came about through joy, sorrow, or mystery. Night and day assumed deep, spiritual meaning, as did the powerful sun, the ever growing and shrinking moon, the rotating pattern of stars, the magic of each season. All this was part of the expanding, never-ending whole.

My own experience has been largely here in New Mexico, though the Southern Utes and the Ute Mountain Utes of Colorado were part of my learning process, too. Since 1961, when I first met a Taos Pueblo medicine man, I've felt as much kinship with the Indians as I feel with ravens, lizards, and coyotes. They—and we—are of the same material, the same essence. It's taken a while to understand that Native American wisdom, so envied by non-Indians, so imitated and so abused, is basically an awareness and appreciation of the complex, magical world around us. Nature, not us, is what keeps on giving.

To the Pueblos of New Mexico, the Twelve Great Paths of the Moon are part of that awareness and appreciation. The moons they watch are the moons of their ancestors and of children yet unborn; they are our moons, too, inviting reflection on our lives and on the alarming condition of the world. For it is not through war or violence that lives and nations are changed, but through application of old, enduring truths. These truths have no label—Christian, Jewish, Muslim, or Buddhist—for they are simply our most basic connection to one another, to origins, and to a future that must contain the promise of ages past.

I offer here my own interpretation of the Twelve Great Paths of the Moon, a series of poems and meditations to help each of us on our journey.

NANCY WOOD
Santa Fe, New Mexico
December 1994

THE TWELVE GREAT PATHS OF THE MOON

A long time ago, when Father Sky took Mother Earth in his arms and mated with her, the Moon was born. As it grew bigger and bigger out there among the basket of stars, the Sun Dogs took turns biting it. Snap, snap, they went, until the Moon looked like this:

The ragged little Moon continued to shine brightly in the sky. Spirit Walker, who guided all the Two-Legged and Four-Legged Creatures at this time, worried about the Moon. She told all the creatures to dance around the plaza, men with Deer, women with Corn, children with Turtles. On the Night When Red Leaves Fell, the creatures looked up. The Moon was growing bigger! It grew and grew until at last it had a full, happy face. But then the Sun Dogs chewed on it again and whittled it down until it looked like this:

From then on, the Two-Legged Creatures and the Four-Legged Creatures got used to the growing and the dying of the Moon. They got used to the Sun Dogs chewing on it and Father Sun casting a black shadow on its round face every once in a while. All the creatures got together and decided to give each of these moons a name, which are today, as they were then:

January, Man Moon: Söenpana
February, Wind Big Moon: Walapana
March, Ash Moon: Naxöpana
April, Planting Moon: Kapana
May, Corn Planting Moon: Iakápana
June, Corn Tassel Coming Out Moon: Kapnákoyapana
July, Sun House Moon: Tultöpana
August, Lake Moon: Paw'epana
September, Corn Ripe Moon: Iaköwapana
October, Leaves Falling Moon: Ölulpana
November, Corn Depositing Moon: Iatayæpana
December, Night Fire Moon: Nuúpapana

Cloud Dreamer

January ☾ *Man Moon* ☾ *Söenpana*

MEDITATION

January's great path of the moon is solitude.

Each day is part of an infinite puzzle, interlocked with all the preceding days and the ones that follow. You will never solve the infinite puzzle until you learn to let go of fear. In letting go of fear, the puzzle fits together; a million separate pieces, yet finally only one—the journey of experience. Alone.

Look for patterns. Why do you take the same road to work every day? Is there another way to get where you are going? Do you have to go at all? Is a day of rest more important than doing what's expected of you? Do you care what others think?

When days are short, memory is long. Remember how rain on pavement smells? Fresh earth, turned over with a shovel? Have you forgotten the slick, peeled look of earthworms? The nakedness of baby birds? Think spring, and you will overcome the dark heart of winter. It's up to you.

Take stock of your life now, while the earth around you sleeps. A new year means a new beginning; a new beginning is an opportunity to bury old mistakes. You can't change a thing through regret, you can only wear yourself out. Within you lies all the courage you need.

Solitude opens all the closed doors, even those nailed shut.

A Blue Sea Rising

Alive Alone

We are all alive alone.
    Neither friend nor lover
Child nor mother
    Can light our way for very long.
Out of loneliness
    Arises the self we never knew.
Out of fear
    Comes the wisdom of our ancestors.
Out of impatience
    Grows the persistence of old age.
These shadows of our memory
    Create new pathways to the soul
    So that in being alive alone
    We become alive together.

Fire Ponies

A Family of Animals

My father was a hunter who wished his feet were hooves
so he could run faster, and his arms
were two front legs to bring him
closer to the earth that spoke his language.

My mother was a sleek, young deer dreaming
in the grass about a boy who would eventually
marry her, and give her the kind of children
who would not disgrace their families.

When my father saw my mother standing there
he drew his bow and let his arrow fly
straight into her heart, which burst open,
and a cloud of pretty flowers came out.

When my father saw that my mother
was a beautiful animal with long legs
much stronger than his own, he lay down
beside her and replaced her heart with his.

After that the hunter and the deer became one
animal and their children became different
animals, some of us fast, some of us slow,
but all of us part of the family of animals.

Woman-Heart Spirit

The woman-heart spirit was released by the Creator
    a long time ago in order to nurture children,
    animals and plants, trees and rocks, and also
men, who resisted the softening of their wild nature.

The woman-heart spirit roamed the deserts and the mountains
    looking for ways to create awareness,
    the food the earth needed for survival,
and the recognition of beauty in the land.

The woman-heart spirit was wild, untamed
    like the river and the wind
    who taught her knowledge of a certain kind,
different from the knowledge of men or children.

The woman-heart spirit became the guardian
    of language and music and the stories
    needed by birds and animals and people, as
the world changed and imagination dried up.

The woman-heart spirit became the keeper of compassion,
    strong yet invisible, the connection between
    all living things. The woman-heart spirit
is nothing more than love, overlooked when the world began.

February ☾ *Wind Big Moon* ☾ *Walapana*

MEDITATION

February's great path of the moon is introspection.

Friends come and go the way lovers often do. Some are only fair blue skies and disappear when the weather changes. A true friend, a true lover, remains even when the sunlight ends. A true friend helps to catch the rain. A false friend says it isn't raining, even when you feel the drops.

How many true friends do you need? One is enough, but four is even better, one for each direction you take:

east: harmony
south: clarity
west: adventure
north: love

Within these four directions are four more, and four more after that. In this way, both knowledge and friends increase at the same time. Indefinitely.

Just because it's winter doesn't mean you can't grow. Remember how everything waits beneath the surface. Nature knows when her time is coming. So do you. Why resist spring just because snow is falling?

Introspection is the key to understanding the conflict raging within you. Dig out the old fear and throw it away. Fill up your soul with pieces of beauty. Take time to knit them together. They will make a whole.

White Hummingbird

Things That Remember Themselves

Things that remember themselves
are not forgotten, but rise on wings
of experience and paint our minds
with the visions of our ancestors.

Things that remember themselves are pictures
without form and words without a tongue.
They give meaning to what we thought
we had forgotten in our youth.

Things that remember themselves give light
to the uncertain paths we used to take,
bringing beauty to the house
of our ripening old age.

The Beginning Time

In the Beginning Time was darkness. No light, just
the hush of the universe, waiting to be born. The Sun Father
came first, torn from the flesh of infinity, hard
and merciless. He created possibility, the first universal truth.
    He mated with the Moon Mother when he had time.

Their children were Earth and all the other planets, even
the Milky Way, which is the Sky Ladder to Beyond. The Sun Father
and the Moon Mother brought harmony, the second universal truth.
They became inseparable, bound by destiny, even though
    One was always chasing the other through the sky.

After a time there was the birth of animals. They were
the same as people. No difference, except some had two legs
and others four. The animals discovered imagination,
the third universal truth. Their stories comforted and protected
    All who heard them, even wind and rain and fire.

The principal animals were the Elk People and the Bear People,
the Coyote People and the Rabbit People, one for each
of the four sacred directions. The Raven People guarded
the World Above and the Badger People the World Below. All these
People came together and created warmth, the fourth universal truth.
    Their fire made illumination possible.

After that, the People divided into clans and spread out.
Their different worlds expanded, each with possibility, harmony, imagination and warmth. When they grew hungry, food was provided, grass or insects or meat, as much as they needed to survive.

Hunger became the fifth universal truth.

Oceans were made, also mountains, rivers, and deserts.
Trees were made, also stones and flowers, even dry dust.
In this way, things began to be noticed. The People discovered beauty, the sixth universal truth. They made gifts of beauty to one another and created happiness, the seventh universal truth.

The circle of life was almost complete.

Then along came strangers and horses from the south.
It was a time of gunpowder and destruction, of trying to protect themselves from fear, the eighth universal truth. Many People died. They lost their homes and food and children. But they survived. When the People got together again, they discovered hope.

They decided that was the greatest truth of all.

Dream Keeper

March ☾ Ash Moon ☾ Naxöpana

MEDITATION

March's great path of the moon is understanding.

Children and dogs are not meant to do what you want them to do. If you tell them to walk straight, they'll run zigzag. If you complain about their friends, they will ignore you. If you want them to stay in, they will want to go out.

So what? What did you do when you were young? Learn to let go of your children at the same time as you plant them in your garden. Give them wings and roots, so they can fly and stay put at the same time. Isn't this what your parents gave you? Did you even know it, then?

You can't change dogs or children. You can only try to understand them. For one hour, put yourself in your child's shoes. See how far you are able to walk before you fall down. As for your dog, try walking on all fours. Try eating without hands. What do you think he's trying to tell you when he barks?

You have many different natures. Light and dark. Kind and mean. Inconsistent and predictable. You'll never be perfect. But you can be better than you are now. For your own sake, try.

Understanding yourself is the first step toward understanding other people. A difficult but necessary step.

Family Tree I

In our village stands an old, old tree,
    its branches sheltering the spirit of our people,
    offering shade and comfort, the whisper of leaves, the
    sacredness of twenty generations alive in mystery.

Long ago the grandfather buried himself in the roots
    of our family tree and there his wisdom found a home.
    He drew strength from rain and sun and company.
And so he grew.

The father expanded within the sacred circle of the trunk
    of our family tree and there his knowledge began.
    A look of endurance formed upon his layer of bark.
And so he grew.

The children arrived as branches growing in all directions,
    some strong, some weak, but each attached
    to the sacred energy of our ancestors.
And so they grew.

The grandchildren appeared as fresh, green leaves,
    hanging on with nothing more than tenacity,
    letting go whenever it was time to fall.
And so they grew.

A long time passed. Then the grandfather spoke to his grandchildren
from his home beneath the earth. He said: What have you learned
about the wind ripping you from your branches every autumn?
The grandchildren answered: The importance of not expecting too much.

Then the grandfather called out to the children who were branches,
bare in winter, full in summer. He said: What have you learned,
my children, out there in the rain, with everything against you?
The children answered: The importance of waiting for next year.

Then the grandfather spoke to the father expanding so slowly that
no one noticed his growth. He said: What have you learned,
my son, about standing in the same spot for years on end?
The father answered: The importance of patience.

When all these lessons were learned, the tree in our village
grew ever taller and more beautiful. People came from miles
around just to look at it and to listen to its many voices.
They said: Without this tree, the landscape would be silent.

Those strangers began to notice shadows and dust and pollen.
They spoke a language that had not been heard
for generations. Those strangers became like family to us.
And so we grew.

Who Sees a Thing Deeper Than the Spirits See?

Who sees a thing deeper than the spirits see?

From his place in the sky, the Hawk looks down on history,
Each war, each baby born, each rising sun,
Belongs to his memory of continuity.

Who sees a thing deeper than the spirits see?

From her cave in the mountains, the Bear embraces winter
And discovers the universe deep within
Her snowy dreams of summer's honey.

Who sees a thing deeper than the spirits see?

In the far ocean's depths, Great Whales carry messages
From a long ago time, when the seeds of birds and animals
Were borne on earth's long umbilical cord.

Who sees a thing deeper than the spirits see?

From his hole in the ground, the Gopher remembers
A time when there was no war and no famine, a time
When the horizon ended at the doorway of his home.

April ☾ Planting Moon ☾ Kapana

MEDITATION

April's great path of the moon is regeneration.

When you thought that spring forgot to come, a meadowlark sang in a tree. A flower popped out of the ground. You felt like dancing. Like singing to the clouds. Now is the time to learn how to breathe all over again. Pretend you are a newborn baby. Get the staleness of winter out of your heart and mind and body. It's time to be reborn as a pocket gopher.

Passing through a time of solitude and introspection makes you realize how precious simple things are. Look around. If the sky seems too low, push it up. If the earth seems too still, put your face in the mud and sing it a growing song. Put wildflowers in your ears. Howl at the next full moon. Talk to coyotes, to ravens, to the little ant digging itself out of the ground. What's the worst thing that can happen?

Ask yourself: Is there enough of you to go around? Do people expect too much? Is your work something you want to do? Or have to do? Do you yearn for a new place? A new person with whom to share your life?

Regeneration allows you to grow wings. Sprout roots. Two more legs. Or fins. Regeneration means that you can start growing all over again, this time from the inside out. There is time for everything, even that which you thought too late to happen.

Night Garden

Making the Tree Bloom

In my part of the world, all was a desert.
 There was no rain for a long time. Sand
 Grew wings and flew around, stinging everything.
 Insects left or became stones. Even
 The wind grew tired and quit blowing.

In my part of the world, we prayed for rain.
 We sang songs to Star Fire and Painted Drum,
 Those children of innocence and expectation.
 We listened for the Voice of Thunder
 And watched for the Rainbow Door.

In my part of the world was silence.
 Nobody breathed. And then we heard
 The Voice That Beautifies the Land, rolling out
 From the Blue Woman of the West who sang
 To storm clouds stuck in a far-off sky.

In my part of the world, a tiny seed dropped
 From the mouth of a bird passing by. And then
 A soft rain fell. The arms of the sun took hold.
 We danced as a tree began to bloom, giving us
 The promise of harvest in our home.

On Being Alive

Ask a snake what it means to be alive,
and it will tell you,
feeling grass on my belly.

Ask a bluebird what it means to be alive,
and it will tell you,
flying high above the world.

Ask a tree what it means to be alive,
and it will tell you,
being rooted in one place.

Ask an ant what it means to be alive,
and it will tell you,
trying not to get stepped on.

Ask a coyote what it means to be alive,
and it will tell you,
being smarter than the rest.

Ask a snail what it means to be alive,
and it will tell you,
going at my own pace.

Ask a river what it means to be alive
and it will tell you,
finding freedom of the wildest kind.

Ask the wind what it means to be alive,
and it will tell you,
blowing whichever way I want.

Ask a meadowlark what it means to be alive,
and it will tell you,
singing the sweetest song I know.

Ask a porcupine what it means to be alive,
and it will tell you,
learning to be by myself.

Ask a rainbow what it means to be alive,
and it will tell you,
spreading beauty around the earth.

Each thing in nature is gloriously alive,
giving us a clear reason
why the Creator put it there.

Crow Owner

May ☾ Corn Planting Moon ☾ Iakápana

MEDITATION

May's great path of the moon is acceptance.

You don't have forever, so why worry about things you cannot change? What bothers you today will not bother you a year from now. You'll wonder what made you so angry. So sad. Perhaps you have to trip over a few more rocks in order to find your direction. Accept it, lying facedown on the earth, until it answers your prayer for meaning.

If those who stand in your way cast a shadow on your life, remember you can always step aside. It's probably sunnier on the other side of the path, anyway. And fewer stones, besides.

Life demands so much. Often so little seems to return, no matter how hard you try. What matters is that you have hope and strength and perseverance. Did you think you would ever be thanked?

What do you do when people hurt you? If you love them, practice kindness. If you don't love them, practice detachment.

Acceptance means you've grown up enough to handle the situation.

Hummingbird

The Voice That Beautifies the Land

The Voice That Beautifies the Land
    is the insistent call of the dove in spring,
    or the movement of rock on the mesa top,
In answer to a rising cloud of butterflies.

The Voice That Beautifies the Land
    is the squeak of corn growing high in summer,
    or the soft kiss of water touching sand
Along the riverbank, where locusts demand to be heard.

The Voice That Beautifies the Land
    is the whisper of dry leaves dancing in the fall,
    or the cry of geese in arrowhead formation,
Saying farewell to the rivers that fed them.

The Voice That Beautifies the Land
    is the murmur of snowflakes in winter,
    or the creak of old trees rising to catch them
As the raven announces the shadow of spring.

The Voice That Beautifies the Land
    is the chorus of clouds bumping into one another,
    or the crack of ice crying out for sun
    as the turtle sings of a new season in the mud.

Paths of the Moon

Two Sisters

Two sisters, dressed in the threads of the universe, lived together
in the sky, with only the sun and the moon for company.
To keep themselves amused, they danced on top of the rainbow.
When they cried, it looked like dew. When they laughed,
Sunlight broke into pieces and covered the earth with turtledoves.

When the two sisters ran across the sky together, their footsteps
echoed like thunder and woke the Creator from his nap.
He saw their beauty and turned them into morning stars. Now
the two sisters greet the sun at dawn, making a path of splendor
Across the disappearing face of darkness in the sky.

Plains Vestige

June ☾ Corn Tassel Coming Out Moon ☾ Kapnákoyapana

MEDITATION

June's great path of the moon is listening.

There is a story inside everything: wind, rain, fire. Even in the sound corn makes when it is trying to grow in the field. Rivers have great stories, so do leaves rustling on trees. Listen to old stones for information about survival. Put a pebble to your ear and listen to the tale it has to tell. What a seashell has to say will surprise you. So, too, will words written on the wind.

Listening to silence is hardest of all. You want to fill it up with conversation. With noise. With distraction. Resist the impulse. In silence you can listen to your own heartbeat; you can take the pulse of continuity. In silence, you can dream great dreams. You can discover your own music.

Why is it harder to let go than it is to hang on? Even when a thing seems finished, a shadow remains. You ask: Did I do right? Was there a way to bury our differences? By saying nothing, did you say all?

It takes effort to make something of your life when other people are making do with less. Have courage to make a change. Indecision prevents action. Memory clouds reason. Fear paralyzes. Routine decays.

Listening means hearing the voice within you. It never fails to tell you the truth, even if you don't want to hear it.

Emergence

The Wild Woman's Lullaby

Wild woman of the mountains, running barefoot through the grass
    of summer, your raven hair braided with sunlight,
    and a touch of mischief in your eyes, sing a song
    of freedom to the dark skies of isolation:

    "I am a bluebird's wing, the voice of fire rising higher
    than the cloud point of summer rain. I am the
    footstep you hear in darkness, leading you out of the
    night. I am forgiveness and creation's daughter."

Wild woman of the mountains, swimming upriver
    against the current, your body covered with leaves,
    the blood of otters flowing in your strong arms,
    sing a lullaby to children yet unborn:

    "I am mother to the whole earth, daughter to the
    falling sky, sister to dreams of rising beyond
    life's ordinary claims. I am you inside of me. I ask:
'Oh, children of the coming generation, how will you live?
Oh, children of war and famine, what will you do for laughter?' "

Only those who hear the voice of the mountain
    can sing the wild woman's lullaby. Only those who run
    barefoot through grass, and swim upriver, can know
    the message in her heart.

Connections

Every time we take a breath, we become
the universe. The very moment of creation
is contained in us and passes on to rocks and trees,
animals and fish. The old ones say the essence of life
is in water and wind, earth and breath, fire and bone,
but most of all in breath, our first connection
to the elk, the hawk, the bear, and the buffalo.
Without breath, no connection.
Without connection, no creation.
Without creation, no breath.
This is the sacred circle of life, unbroken.

July ☾ Sun House Moon ☾ Tultöpana

MEDITATION

July's great path of the moon is passion.

How do you know if the one you love is true? Because he says so? Because he showers you with gifts? Takes you dancing? Makes promises sound like plans? Perhaps he is just as afraid as you.

Your love is true if he listens to your heartbeat. If he stops and picks a wildflower and sees your eyes in every petal. That is passion.

Your love is true if he says your name like poetry, like wind, like fire. Like the last breath of summer, yielding to the fall. That is passion.

Passion is also dedication to something you believe in, whether it be a kind of learning, work that matters to you, or simply life itself.

In the autumn of my life, I fell in love for the first time, though I had been fooled many times before. He was sun and moon and stars to me, the voice of the rock, reaffirming the old songs I used to sing alone. We danced together in moonlight, climbed the highest mountains, walked through rain, saw beauty everywhere. He made me larger than I am; I made him see a clearer path. We became like two trees growing from a common root; we made each other possible.

Passion is what you give to what matters most to you.

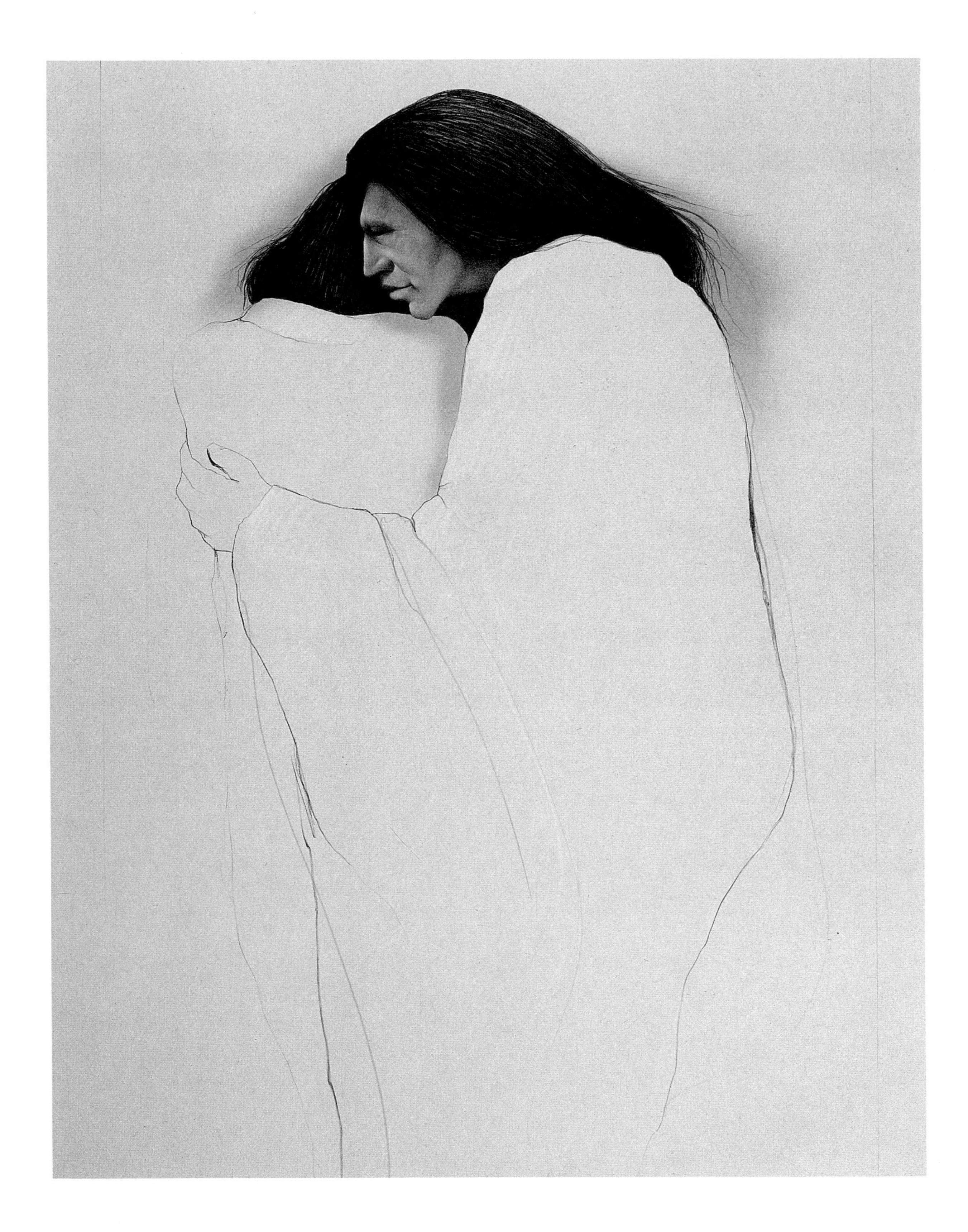

Sisters

Love Song

I shall see you again, if the world lasts, even though
you are gone from my sight. My breath creates
new life for you, now that we are apart and
the universe lies here in the ashes of my memory.

I shall see you again, if the world lasts, in the nighttime sky,
where even the separated stars move together
in the same direction. As moon follows sun, so shall I
follow you across our star-lined path, the one we created

Together. Do you remember? Come, my love, and find me
crying on a mountaintop, where my tears
make new flowers bloom. Come run with me through
dreaming fields and catch rainbow colors for our eyes,

The way we used to. Our holy place is holy still;
our love is not diminished by absence or by pain.
Death has but interrupted our loving, and I know
I shall see you again, if the world lasts.

Messenger

Invitation to Life

I invite you to life
        and you send regrets.
        Sorry can't come, too late or
        too soon, too busy, too scared,
Too much involved in the business of living.

The reasons you give
        are a song all their own.
        off-key and shallow, with the sound
        of avoidance, the rhythm
Familiar, the words echoing the same old excuses.

I'll issue no more invitations
        to you. The party's been
        cancelled, the guests won't arrive
        in time to find me having
A dance all my own. You see,

I invited myself to my life
        and finally accepted.

Why Flowers Smell the Way They Do

When flowers were first invented, they smelled like mud.
    Dust shook out of their petals and no one
    wanted to be around them for very long,
the rose especially. It smelled like dead leaves.

In those days there were order and grace
    and predictability. Except for flowers,
    beautiful yet unnoticed, things were what
they were intended to be. Birds were just birds and

Trees were just trees. Caterpillars crawled along
    and the meadowlark could be counted on to sing
    the way he was supposed to. Flowers refused
to smell good because they thought no one loved them.

So it was, for a long time. Then one day a beautiful
    girl picked a wild rose and put it in her hair,
    so boys would admire her as she passed by.
    Sniff, sniff, they went, and turned to watch her.

One boy said: The smell of that wild rose makes me
    want to fall in love. The other boys came closer
    and smelled the rose. They all agreed. The flower
    smelled sweet and made them fall in love, too.
From that day on, flowers began to smell the way they do now.
    Especially the wild rose, worn in a pretty girl's hair.

August ☾ Lake Moon ☾ Paw'epana

MEDITATION

August's great path of the moon is change.

Fate and opportunity often look alike. So do generosity and guilt. The place where these four friends meet is called life. You must make the most of your life. To do less is to fail yourself. No one else is to blame for your indecision or mistakes. Everything comes from the courage of experience.

You can't catch sunlight by staying indoors. You can't recognize quality if you settle for imitation. If you are not in the right place, leave. If you are not doing work that matters, quit. If life is not what you want it to be, change. If you are surrounded by false friends, trade them for new ones, the quiet, steady kind. If something nags at your heart, open it up and have a look. What you find there may surprise you.

How do you become strong?

Throw your importance away. Make friends with trees. Sing a song with a mourning dove. Crawl along the ground with a snake. Do push-ups with a lizard. Learn the language of squirrels. Decipher the meaning of old stones. Find wisdom in a baby's eyes. Look at an old man as if he were new.

Change means growth. Growth is necessary for trees and other living things. Without growth, nothing would be harvested, except doubt.

Teton Trade Beads

The Beads of Life

The space between events is where
most of life is lived. Those half-remembered moments
of joy or sadness, fear or disappointment, are merely
beads of life strung together
to make one expanding necklace of experience.

The space between events is where
we grow old. From sunrise to sunset one day lives
as another day emerges from the fluid womb of dawn,
the first bead strung upon
the everlasting thread of life.

The space between events is where
knowledge marries beauty. In quiet reflection
we remember only the colored outline of events,
the black and white of war, the rosiness
that surrounded our first love.

The space between events is why
we go on living. The laughter of a child or
the sigh of wind in a canyon becomes the music
we hear expanding in our hearts each time
we gather one more bead of life.

Spring Matrix

In the Garden of the House God

Tame roses grow in my garden these days, not the
wild variety of my youth, the thorny kind that used to
give me pain even as I admired their beauty. My house
is bare of all the old vines that used to choke me and now

I cultivate only the rare flowers of my old age. In the garden
of the House God, I pray for strength to last me to
the end and for my path to be free of weeds, because
I have no room for unwelcome visitors anymore.

The earth is rich in my garden these days. Seeds of
contentment have sprouted out of my old fear, and
the dryness of summer has become the ripeness
with which I fill my days. In the garden of the House God,

The tame rose blooms at last.

Gathering Sunbeams

The way to gather sunbeams is carefully, making sure
they do not break or become
mere shadows of your uncertainty.

The way to gather sunbeams is hopefully, bending
to catch the light between your fingers
before storm clouds devour opportunity.

The way to gather sunbeams is crazily, putting
them in your pocket if you catch any,
laughing at their feeling of mobility.

The way to gather sunbeams is joyfully, keeping
step with the dance they do across the earth,
drawing you into their world of fragility.

September ☾ *Corn Ripe Moon* ☾ *Iakö̈wapana*

MEDITATION

September's great path of the moon is awareness.

Lie down in a secret place with your head pointed toward the east and stay there until you learn something. Then move slowly to the south, facedown. Notice what is in front of your nose: leaves, pine needles, dirt, insects, pebbles. When you turn to the west, dig into the earth with your fingers. Smell the richness of history. Imagine what this spot was like ten thousand years ago. Who came this way before you? Do they speak to you? Watch the way shadows move. It's history stirring.

Now turn to the north and stay there until you can imagine every drop of rain, every flake of snow that has fallen there. Imagine the animals that have walked by; the snakes and insects and rodents who live nearby; the plants and trees that grow; the earthquakes and the floods, the blizzards and the heat. Imagine fire and drought. Think of how the earth endures.

Complete the circle with your body. Turn to the east and listen for the Voice That Awakens the Land. When you hear it and know what it means, turn over and look at the sky. Think of everything that has happened there. The birth and death of stars. The rising and setting of moon and sun. The birds that have flown by, the clouds that have formed in various shapes and sizes and colors. Consider the darkness beyond.

All time, all place is present in these two circles, expanding from your body in both directions, above and below. These two circles finally join together in the sky. It's called the seam of life.

Just think: In these circles, you have created your own universe. That's what awareness is all about.

River Genesis

The Center of the World

Anywhere is the center of the world.
  A garden where one seed gives birth
  to a whole harvest of imagination.
Anywhere is the center of the world.
  A house where walls expand
  to encompass the waiting land.
Anywhere is the center of the world.
  A heart that sings old songs,
  A spirit that remembers old dreams.
Anywhere is the center of the world.
  The place where my love lives.
  The house we made of earth.
  The dream we built on hope.
  The spirit that connects our tongues
  To songs of ancient wisdom.

Family Tree II

An old woman in our village became a tree root when she died. All alone beneath the earth, with no sunlight and no relatives, she was lonely. She cried out for company. High in the sky, the birds heard her and brought her some seeds. Then the storm clouds heard her and sent rain. When the rain was over, the seed and the root took hold of one another. They mated endurance to potential. The result was that something began to open.

Soon a tender green shoot grew out of the earth, fragile yet strong as a woman. It had the beauty of a young girl and the patience of an old grandmother. Rain and sun made it grow. Birds sang songs to help it along. Animals stopped by to peer at it. They waited while the earth expanded.

After a while the tender green shoot began to look like a sapling. Branches formed so birds would have a place for their nests; leaves grew so animals would have shade. Out of the leaves came a song. The wind carried it out across the land and it became universal. Everyone hummed along.

Deep beneath the earth, the old grandmother root spoke: I am the one who is holding you up, she said. Without me, you would blow down.

That's true, the beautiful young tree said. But I give meaning to your memory. I am living testimony to your unseen presence. The wind shook the branches and made a new song with the leaves. It was laughter.

The old grandmother root said: Well, it's about time the younger generation recognized the importance of us old people. We are still useful.

The tree shook in the wind. Deep beneath the earth, the old grandmother root felt the vibration. And she began to dance right there in her dark place. She imagined she had sunlight and all her relatives for company. After that, she was never lonely again, because she knew that her granddaughter was part of her forever, growing stronger and more beautiful every day.

October ☾ Leaves Falling Moon ☾ Öulpana

MEDITATION

October's great path of the moon is respect.

For us, the new year begins now and not in January. This is a time of sleeping seeds and birds flying south for the winter. Leaves begin to fall; the sun turns pale in the sky. It is the Moon of Putting Away and the Moon of Remembering Old Names. Preparation begins for the coming winter. We look for signs of whether it will be a hard winter: Do the clouds have long tails? Does the chipmunk work harder, storing food for winter? Does ice have an early voice? What does the raven say? Does the coyote change his song? Do our hearts stir with warning?

Now is a time to learn respect for all living things—even for those who are not your friends. Is there a voice from your past that you didn't pay attention to? Take time to mend broken connections. Find out why someone does not like you; respect that person even so.

Respect starts on the simplest level. Walk to the mountains where the first snow has already fallen. Notice that the stream has a collar of ice along the edges. Dry leaves move on the wind, sighing. Inside you, something calms down. Turn your face to the sun: For everything in the past, thank you. To the future, yes.

Respect is a matter of equality, even in the worst of times.

Red Mountain Morning

Looking at Mountains

Mountains that are looked at have a particular grace,
some are rounded and gentle, others have a wildness
of spirit, the sharp rock face of invincibility.
Still others beckon with deceptive calm, luring the unwary
with their raw beauty, heads buried in clouds, sunlight
dancing on meadows like sky fingers. The great rock god
Of the mountains sleeps with one eye open to catch eagles
and elk, wind and rainbows, the strong of limb who climb
those peaks because a mountain lives inside them.

Mountains that are looked at look back with the pleasure
of old women locked in the gaze of new admirers,
so glad for attention, so wary of strangers. Mountains
That are looked at increase in beauty from so much looking
and live on in memory long after we are gone from them,
remembering the hint of immortality there and the way
We were possessed by rock. Mountains that are looked at
look back with authority and the promise of tomorrow,
which is why some people die for them.

Spirit Brothers

We are all one.
    The human and the hummingbird
    The wild horse and the weasel
    The house cat and the red-tailed hawk
    The buffalo and the dog
    The coyote and the cottontail.
The human spirit and the animal spirit
    Grow from a common root
    of understanding.
Human dreams and animal dreams
    Share the limitless horizon
    of our precious mother earth.
The human spirit and the animal spirit
    Join where the circle of the sky
    meets the circle of the earth.
In this sacred space lies the meaning of the universe.
The meaning of the universe is nothing more
    than the appearance of dew on a leaf or
    the dance of light on water, even
    the conversation between two dogs or
    the way a hummingbird flies.

November ☾ *Corn Depositing Moon* ☾ *Iatayæpana*

MEDITATION

November's great path of the moon is mortality.

The sun falls lower in the sky each day. The earth has turned the color of buckskin and gone to sleep. I have been to the cemetery to talk to my ancestors. I left them food to eat, water to drink, thoughts to comfort them. When my turn comes, will I be ready? What if I don't want to die?

I built a house once. Its walls were strong and thick; there were windows on all sides that let in sunlight. The roof stood up under heavy snow and rain. I lived in this house a long time, then I moved away. I had children once. They were good children, though it seemed they would never grow up. Now they are gone. Their toys are put away. Their rooms have been swept clean. I see their faces in my dreams. That time is past; it is another time now. Soon my children will be as old as I am now.

I am alone, yet not alone. If God exists, it is a spirit that runs through me every moment, filling me with awe and caution, appreciation and the gift of creativity. I must be thankful for what is and stop thinking about what is not.

If you had the opportunity, what in your life would you do differently? How would you choose your mate? Your lover? Your friends? Would you build a good house if you knew you had to leave it?

Mortality is the recognition of each day's purpose.

Elk Dreamer

Migration

Going from this place to another place
 requires surrender of your old ways,
 the honoring of sacred wisdom and not
 anticipation of the journey only. The soul's
Migration between the old place and the new means
 that you must recognize your path
 to an unknown destination, risking all
 with the chance of gaining nothing. You are merely
The connection between growth and suffocation,
 the link that joins possibility to pain,
 and thus you become the keeper of your own flame.
Going from this place to another place is like
 the bird in winter who remembers
 the beauty of her springtime nest
 just to keep herself from freezing.

Turquoise Earring

The House of Evening Light

In the house of evening light, I remember the day,
how each moment unfolded and took wing,
touching all that went before and all
That came after. Not one single moment, but
a combination of moments and changing shadows.

In the house of evening light, I watch my life unfold,
from the rosy dawn of anticipation to the heat
of the noonday sun, blazing a path I was afraid
To follow because my heart was closed to the danger
that living a full life brings.

In the house of evening light, I watch
as darkness falls, and one by one familiar faces
fade from my poor vision, and events
That seemed so important this morning now wait
for the mouth of time to swallow them.

In the house of evening light, a star appears,
guiding me toward a new horizon without
the limitation of day's full light or
Those false promises of clouds without rain.
Tomorrow a new heart rises with the sun.

Old Age Dreaming

When I look at you now in winter, I do not see the lines
upon your face or the whiteness of your hair.
The burden of living so full a life is reflected
In your eyes, into which I alone bring light
each time I say, thank you for your precious gifts,
so rich, so rare I never noticed where
Springtime went, only that I spent each season
here, alive with you. And that
is the dream of this old bear caught
Between the jaws of winter, who remembers only
the sweet, warm promise of honey.

December ☾ Night Fire Moon ☾ Nuúpapana

MEDITATION

December's great path of the moon is suffering.

Out of suffering comes compassion for people we never noticed before, the ones in a crowd whose eyes we cannot meet. Out of suffering comes appreciation of what was overlooked before: a sunset, a dawn, a butterfly, the delicate movement of light on a wall. How long does anything last?

What is the nature of your suffering? Illness or accident? Something you did not do right? It is too late for regret. If the stones of suffering are too heavy, drop them. If pain is unbearable, imagine another world of white light. Pink blossoms. A gently flowing stream. Music. The laughter of children. Make yourself live in this imaginary place until the pain moves on.

There is a reason for your suffering. Pain is part of the lesson. Tell it to scour your heart. Pain is a way to acquire new eyes and ears. To be quiet when you have always spoken. To take a journey when you'd rather stay at home. To do with your hands one thing that you are really proud of. Pain will make it beautiful. Pain makes reality possible.

This day is a gift. Do not waste a single moment. Hold snow in your hand until it melts. Notice the color of the sky. Listen to the wind. Watch a bird flying south. Smell winter on the wind. Suffering is the transformation of the self into a sharper, clearer world. There, loving kindness begins.

Touching the Sun

Dancing Moons

Deep in the sanctuary of my loneliness,
I looked at the nighttime sky where
The full moon in its own deep solitude
Suddenly began to dance across the stars.
From dark horizon to dark horizon it went,
Giving light to my silent, shuttered heart,
And to itself the promise of desire.

As I watched, the full moon danced the night away,
Bathed in earth's reflected harmony. Then
The moon became two moons, multiplying on and on
Until the sky was filled with dancing moons.
Those distant orbs of spirited light vanished the moment
The sun came up, yet shadows of their beauty remained,
Reminding me of the blessings of my life.

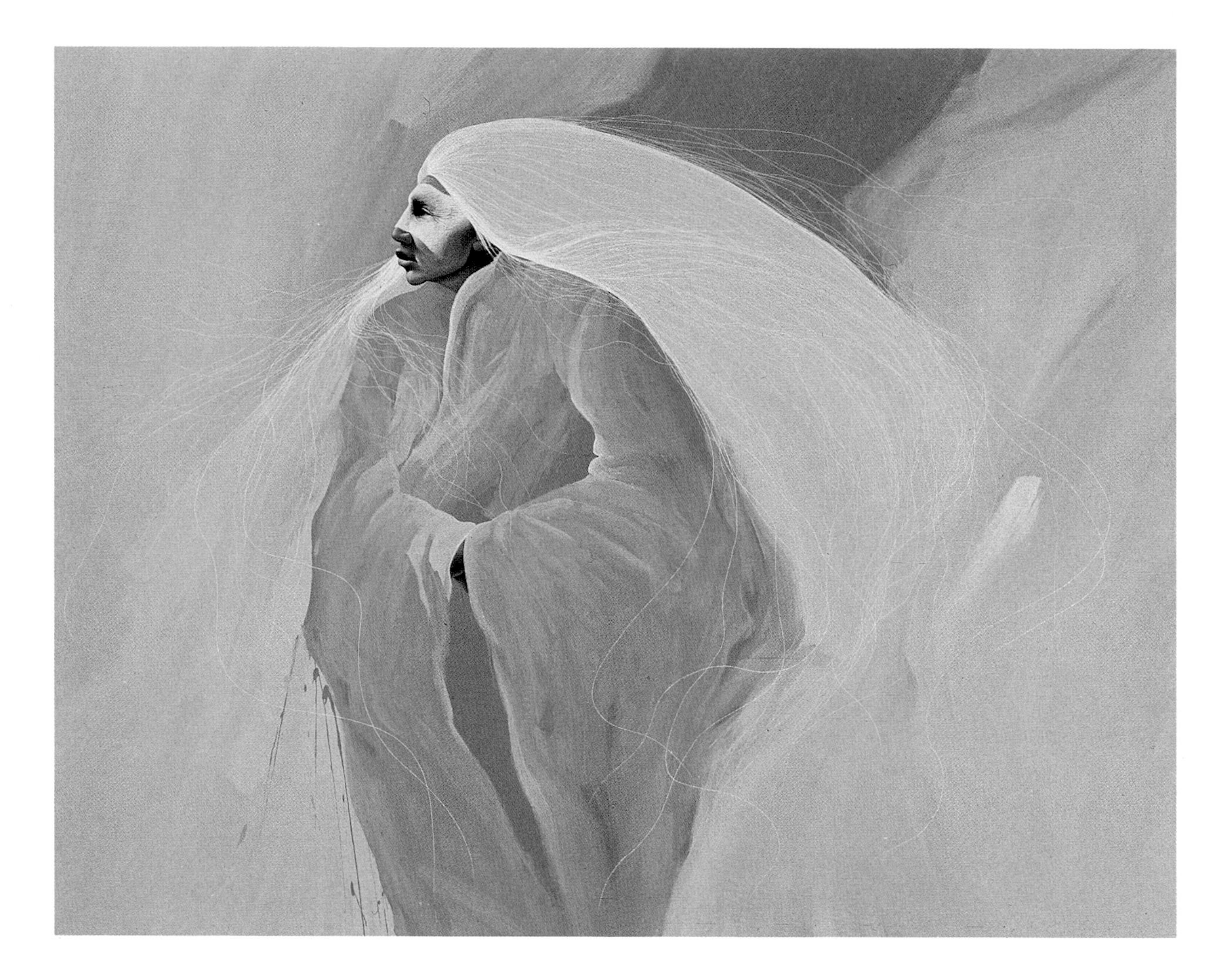

Wounded Knee Winter

The Rainbow Door

When the Rainbow Door opens, the Twelve Great Paths of the Moon
become visible, each one connected like spokes
to the vast moving hub of the universe.
Each Great Path of the Moon contains the blood of our ancestors,
the scattered corn pollen from which
ideas and animals were born.

When the Rainbow Door opens, I see my strength reflected
in ten million stars, in the long drawn net of the Milky Way,
and in the deep changing face of the sky.
The Twelve Great Paths of the Moon unfold through the darkness
of my mind, pulling me beyond Earth's frail claims
into the richness of my dreams.

Beyond the Rainbow Door lies the affirmation of self,
the death of ignorance, the renewal of peace,
and the connected memory of all living things.

In this hallowed place, life begins anew.
In this hallowed place, I am the continuous breath
of all that has gone before
and all that follows after.

Night Fire

The cold of winter makes a fire in my heart and fills my ears
with the music of the meadowlark. Here in my house, made
of the memory of summer and the desire for green grass,
I know that loneliness will never kill me.
Here in a room filled with sorrow for all the world in pain,
I know that fear can never blind me from seeing
eagles rising from the ashes of my fire.
Asleep in a bed covered with longing for spring,
I know that anger never soothed my heart nor
silence solved the problems of my world.
In my dreams I see a perfect little flower, and then I know
that love will heal most anything,
my loneliness included.

Emergence

INDEX OF TITLES

What You Never Knew About Fingers, Forks, & Chopsticks

BY **Patricia Lauber** ILLUSTRATED BY **John Manders**

Simon & Schuster Books for Young Readers

We all need to eat. The first step in eating is to bring food to your mouth, but how you do this depends on where you live. In some parts of the world, people use their fingers. In other societies, they use chopsticks. In still others, they use forks, knives, and spoons for most foods and fingers for some. Each society has rules about the proper way to eat.

Fingers have always been with us. But chopsticks, forks, knives, and spoons have not. These utensils had to be invented. The inventing began in a time called the Stone Age.

Back to Nature—and also back to the Stone Age. . . .

In the Stone Age...

The name *Stone Age* describes a time when tools were made of stone. It began hundreds of thousands of years ago and ended when people discovered metal. This discovery took place at different times in different parts of the world. In a few places, there are still tribes that do not use metal.

Early Stone Age people ate by tearing at food with teeth and nails. But later people discovered flint, a kind of stone that often has a sharp edge.

We can only guess how Stone Age people happened to think of using flint. Perhaps...

A chunk of flint could be used for cutting meat and for scraping hides. By slashing a big chunk of cooked meat, people could make pieces that were easy to pick off. Or they could hack raw meat into small pieces for cooking.

A forked stick was perfect for cooking small pieces of meat without also cooking the fingers.

As time passed, people learned to chip flint into many shapes. They discovered how to make long, thin, pointed blades—the world's first knives.

They made containers for water out of animal skins or bark. To heat water, they dropped hot stones into the containers. Then they could cook grains.

Stone Age people also invented the spoon.

They made spoons out of shells, bone, and horn. They carved a hollow in a chip of wood, which then served as a spoon.

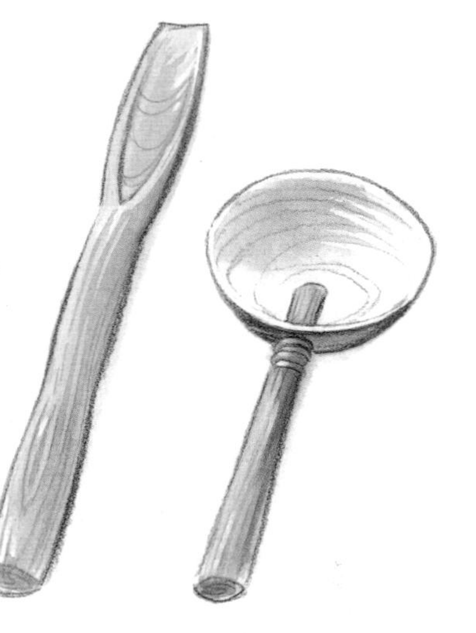

By 9,000 years ago, people were making pottery containers by firing clay in ovens, or kilns. They cooked stews and soups in pots and ate with spoons.

For most of the Stone Age, people moved around to find food, hunting animals and gathering plants. Nine or ten thousand years ago, some people of the Near East discovered farming. Now they could raise food and live in one place. Settlements took shape.

In the Bronze Age...

About 5,500 years ago, another big change took place. People discovered metal. Their first metal was copper. They found lumps of copper, which they could hammer and shape into objects. Next, they somehow discovered how to get copper out of certain rocks by heating them. Perhaps...

Copper was soft, but when mixed with tin, it made the hard metal we call bronze. With this discovery the Bronze Age began. Metal knives and spoons came into use. In time, people discovered other metals—iron and steel, gold, silver.

Bamboo chopsticks of about 4,500 years ago

Meanwhile, far to the east, people had discovered a different way to eat—with chopsticks. No one knows how chopsticks were invented, but perhaps, about 5,000 years ago...

It was a great idea. Soon everyone was using a pair of sticks to handle hot food.

By about 2,500 years ago, when a great civilization was rising in China, the sticks had become the chopsticks we know. They were used to eat everything except soup, which was eaten with an earthenware spoon. Most food was cut with knives into bite-size pieces in the kitchen. But sometimes a whole fish or big piece of meat was served. It was so tender that pieces could be picked off with chopsticks.

Chinese spoons are flat on the bottom.

In time, the use of chopsticks spread to other parts of Asia. Most chopsticks were made of wood, bone, or ivory.

Modern chopsticks are square at one end for easy gripping and round at the other.

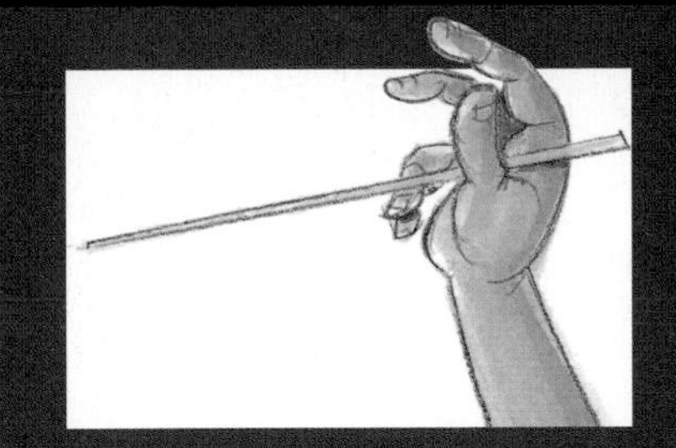

Place one chopstick in your hand. This chopstick should not move.

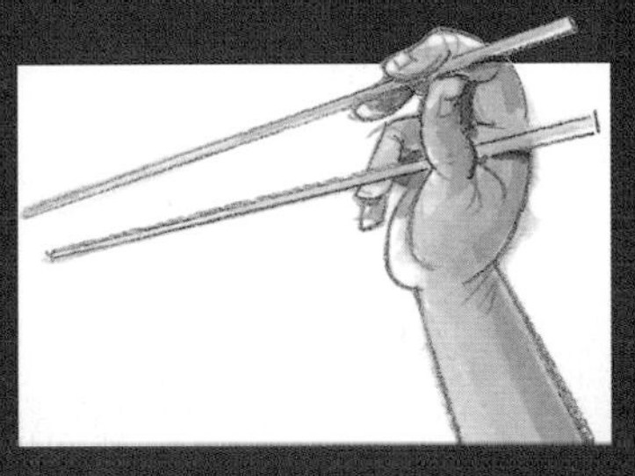

Hold the second like this. Make sure the tips are even.

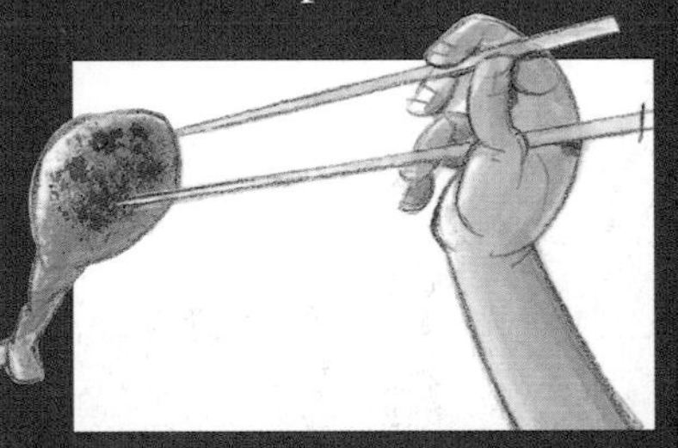

Move the second chopstick to hold food against the first.

Do not let the chopsticks cross.

Ancient Civilizations—Rome

To the west, many changes were taking place as farming spread from the Near East to North Africa and Europe. The first towns took shape, supplied with food from farms. Townspeople worked at trades and in arts and crafts. Over a span of some 6,000 years, great civilizations rose in Egypt, Greece, Rome. Rich people feasted at banquets. They ate with knives, spoons, and fingers, washing their fingers in silver finger bowls and drying them on large linen napkins.

Both the Romans and the Greeks had large kitchen forks with two prongs, or tines. These were used to lift meat out of boiling liquid and to hold meat steady for carving. But there were no table forks.

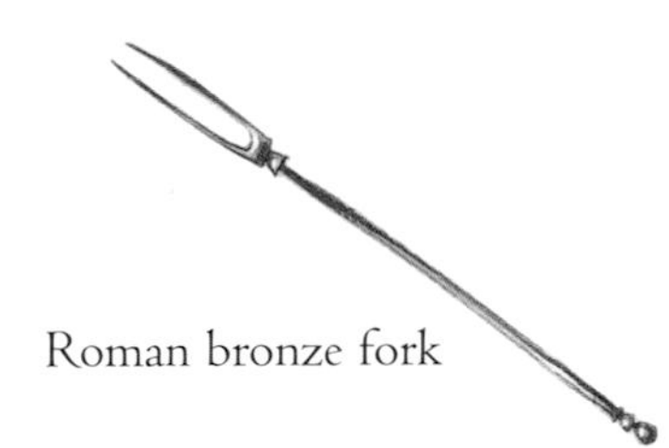

Roman bronze fork

Late in Roman times, napkins became the first doggy bags.

Egyptian bronze knife,
Roman gold spoon, and
Greek ladle with swan handle

Rome was the last of these three great civilizations. At its height, the Roman Empire stretched from Britain in the north to Central Asia in the east. The empire fell around the year 476, attacked by tribes from the north and east.

In the Middle Ages...

In Europe, the thousand years after the Fall of Rome is known as the Middle Ages, because it lies in the middle—between ancient times and modern times. One of the things that happened during the Middle Ages was the Crusades. These were expeditions made by European Christians, who hoped to recover the Holy Land from the Muslims. The Crusades took place between the years 1000 and 1300.

In the Middle Ages ordinary people ate plain meals. Some ate with fingers alone. Others used spoons, knives, and fingers.

The upper classes enjoyed banquets.

A banquet table was set with spoons and soup bowls, one bowl for every two guests. One drinking glass was passed around the table. There were no plates. Instead, each guest used a thick slice of stale bread, called a trencher. Guests brought their own knives. The same knives were also weapons, so they had to be handled carefully. A wrong move might seem a threat.

The knights of the Crusades followed strict rules of behavior. Their behavior stirred an interest in manners. Books of manners, or etiquette, appeared. Among other things, people learned how to behave at the table.

Readers were told:

1. An upper-class person eats with three fingers, not five.

2. A gnawed bone should never be put back on the serving platter. Lay it on the table or throw it on the floor.

3. Do not put your face in your food, snort, or smack your lips while eating.

4. Do not lick your greasy fingers or wipe them on your coat. Wipe them on the tablecloth.

5. Do not put your whole hand in the pot. Do take the first piece of meat or fish that you touch.

6. Do not blow your nose on the tablecloth or wipe it on your sleeve.

Medieval daggers

New customs arose. One paired a knight and a lady at banquets. Each couple shared food and a drinking glass.

In the Renaissance...

In the 1300s, a great age of discovery and exploration was born in western Europe. Learning was prized. The arts blossomed. The time known as the Renaissance, or rebirth, had arrived. It would last 200 years and set the stage for modern times.

Ways of eating changed.

Finally...the Fork

The biggest change of all was the table fork. Table forks had long been used in royal courts of the Middle East, but they reached the West only around the year 1100. At that time, an Italian story says, a nobleman from Venice married a Turkish princess. The princess brought table forks to Venice.

Before long, the princess fell ill and died.

But all her own fault for eating with forks.

Sad, very sad.

Another 200 years passed before nobles in Italy started to use forks.

Italian Renaissance fork

In the 1500s, forks reached the royal court of France. Many thought forks silly.

Even so, forks spread to wealthy homes all over France. By the end of the Renaissance, they had reached Britain, where nobles and other wealthy people began to use them.

These early forks had only two tines. They were fine for holding or spearing meat, but not so good for peas.

The Knife Loses Its Point

Still another change lay ahead. For many years, people had carried their own knives when they traveled or went out to dinner. They cut and speared food with knives. At the end of a meal, many picked their teeth with knives. But the same knives served as weapons.

In 1669, Louis XIV, king of France, decided that there were too many stabbings. He ordered that knives were to have rounded ends. Louis also became the first person in Europe to offer guests a place setting of knives, forks, and spoons.

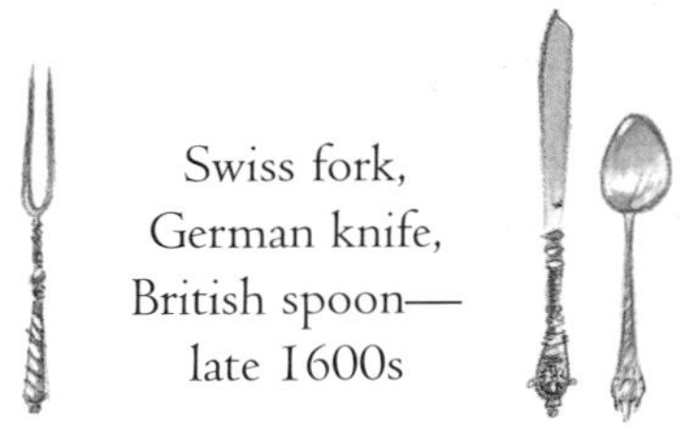

Swiss fork, German knife, British spoon—late 1600s

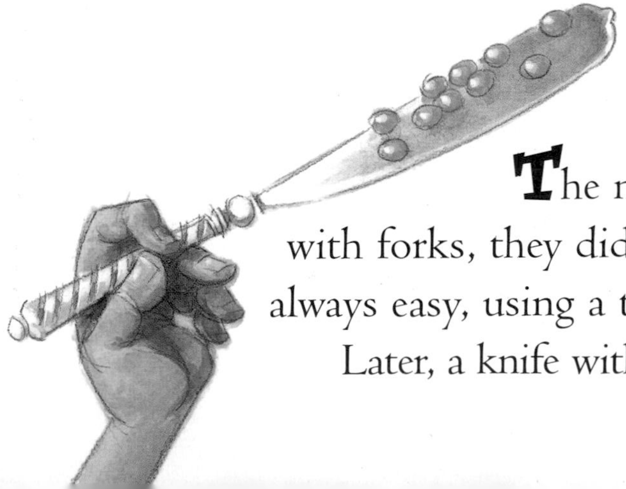

The new style of knife spread. Now that upper-class people were eating with forks, they did not need to spear their food with a knife. Even so, eating was not always easy, using a two-tined fork and a round-ended knife.

Later, a knife with a broader end made it simple to scoop up peas and other loose foods.

In the Eighteenth Century...

By the 1700s, well-to-do people were ordering sets of silver flatware for their tables. The changes called for new books on table manners. Young people were told that they should always:

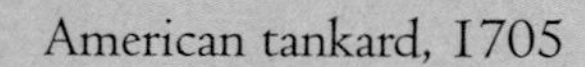

American tankard, 1705

1. Use a napkin, a plate, a spoon, a knife, and a fork at table.

2. Use the napkin to wipe lips and fingers—and never, ever to rub the teeth clean or to blow the nose.

3. Use a fork for lifting meat to the mouth so as not to touch anything greasy with the fingers.

4. And never try to eat soup with a fork.

Across the Atlantic Ocean, the British colonies were not so up-to-date.

By the mid-1700s, Americans were ordering and using forks, but they did not eat the way Europeans did. Europeans kept a fork in the left hand while cutting and lifting food from the plate. Americans ate as they had with spoons—cutting off a piece of meat, then passing the fork to the right hand. Most Americans still eat this way.

Not everybody liked to eat with a fork. Some much preferred to eat off a knife. But the fork was here to stay. New forks had three or four tines, and the tines had a slight curve. They were much easier to eat with.

American fork, 1771-1800

In the Late Nineteenth Century...

At first only the rich had sets of table utensils. Poor people ate with spoons, knives, and fingers. But times were changing. Factories sprang up in Europe and America and turned out large quantities of table utensils, which had once been made by hand. Prices fell. Almost everyone could now afford knives, forks, and spoons.

More and more kinds of table utensils were invented. By the late 1800s, there were almost too many to count.

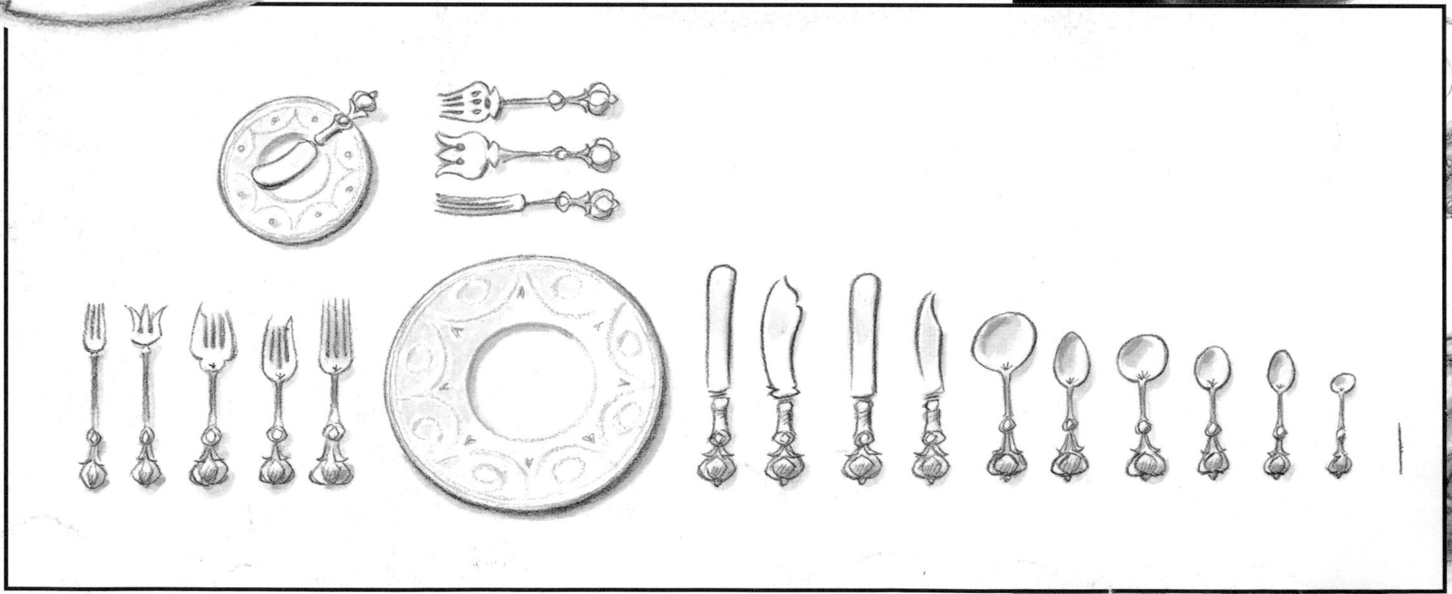

A fancy dinner was not everyone's idea of fun.
I wonder which fork I should use.
I'll watch the hostess and do what she does.
Yes, early people ate like pigs. But they were HAPPY pigs.
I wish I'd stayed home.

Modern Times...
Gross! What a pig!
You're not coming to my birthday party!
Yuk!

Today even fancy dinners are much simpler. At home most tables are set with only a few utensils. It's a good idea to use them and eat neatly so that other people can enjoy their food.

Some foods are eaten with fingers—but in America and western Europe, most eating is done with forks, knives, and spoons.

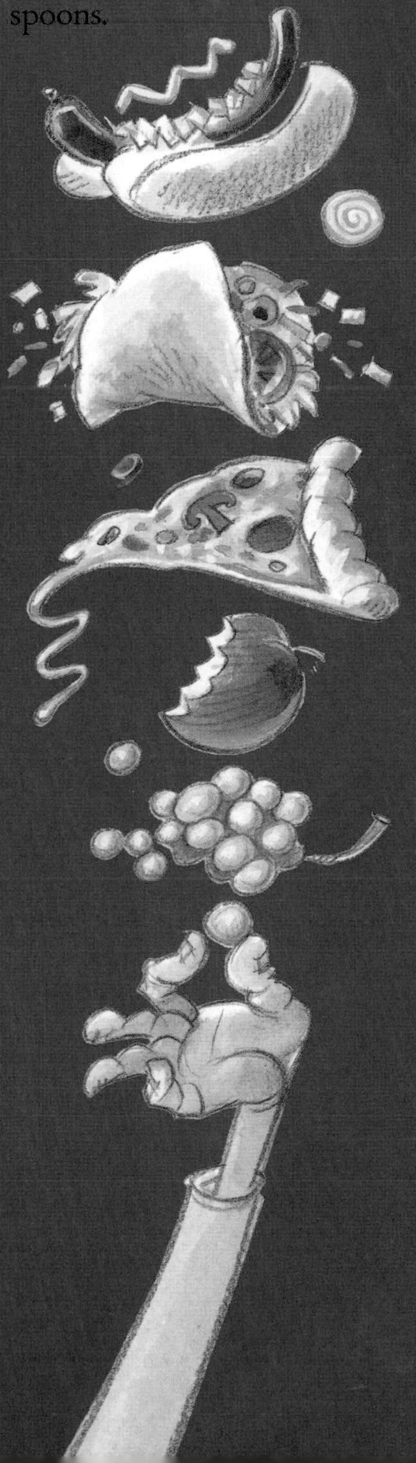

In Other Lands...

In other lands, you may meet people who eat in other ways. If you are a guest, it's polite to eat the way your hosts do.

Some Eskimos eat in the old way. They gather around a stewpot in their igloo, reach in with their hands, and pull out pieces of meat. Men eat first.

Some Arab families also eat with their fingers. They wash their hands, then use only the first three fingers of the right hand to eat. After dining, they wash their hands again.

In India many people also eat with their fingers. In the north, diners use only the fingertips of the right hand. In the south, they use the fingers of both hands. Both groups wash their hands before and after eating.

Japan is one of the countries where people eat with chopsticks.

In today's world, the largest number of people eat with fingers or chopsticks. The smallest number eat with knives, forks, and spoons. Each group has its own rules for eating nicely.

Some Table Manners for Today's Very Refined People

1. Cut food into small bites.

2. Do not eat and drink at the same time.

3. Do not throw a gnawed bone on the floor. Leave it on your plate.

4. Do not put your face in your food, snort, or smack your lips while eating.

5. Use fingers only for finger foods.

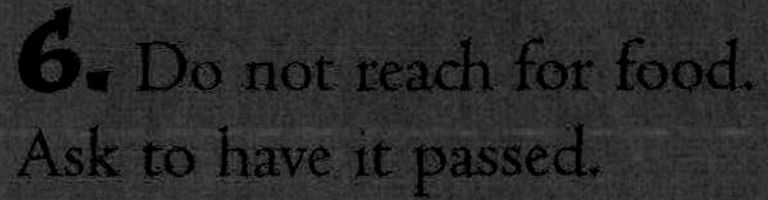

6. Do not reach for food.
Ask to have it passed.

8. Do not lick your greasy fingers or wipe them on the tablecloth. Use your napkin.

7. Chew with your mouth shut—
do not talk and chew.

9. Sit up. Keep elbows off the table.

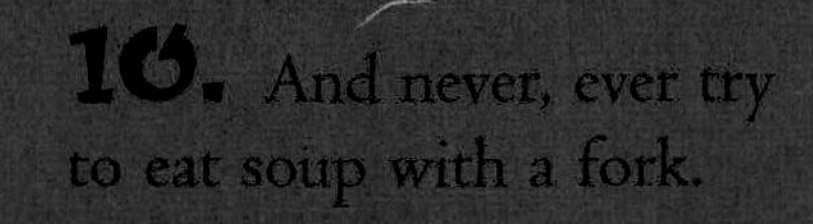

10. And never, ever try to eat soup with a fork.

But sometimes it's fun to get away from it all, back to Nature…

and back to the Stone Age.

Bibliography

Barry, Ann. "The French at Table, From Celts to Now," *The New York Times,* December 4, 1985.

Braudel, Fernand. *The Structures of Everyday Life: The Limits of the Possible.* New York: Harper & Row, 1981.

Deetz, James. *In Small Things Forgotten: The Archeology of Early American Life.* Garden City, New York: Anchor Books, 1977.

* Giblin, James Cross. *From Hand to Mouth: Or, How We Invented Knives, Forks, Spoons, and Chopsticks & the Table Manners to Go with Them.* New York: Thomas Y. Crowell, 1987.

Greer, William R. "Table Manners: A Casualty of the Changing Times," *The New York Times,* October 16, 1985.

Martin, Judith. *Miss Manners' Guide to Excruciatingly Correct Behavior.* New York: Atheneum, 1982.

Needham, Joseph. *The Shorter Science and Civilization in China.* Abridged by Colin A. Ronan. New York: Cambridge University Press, 1978.

Nelson, Bryce. "Some Reflections on the Technology of Eating," *The New York Times,* August 17, 1983.

Petroski, Henry. *The Evolution of Useful Things.* New York: Vintage Books, 1994.

Stern, Philip van Doren. *Prehistoric Europe: From Stone Age Man to the Early Greeks.* New York: W. W. Norton and Company, Inc., 1969.

Tannahill, Reay. *Food in History.* New York: Stein and Day, 1973.

Visser, Margaret. *The Rituals of Dinner: The Origins, Evolution, Eccentricities, and Meaning of Table Manners.* New York: Grove Weidenfeld, 1991.

Weiner, Debra. "Chopsticks: Ritual, Lore and Etiquette," *The New York Times,* December 26, 1984.

* indicates a book written for young readers

To Mom and Dad, who encouraged my youthful obsession with drawing.
—J. M.

Artist's Note

After spending time in the library doing research, I begin an illustration with a sketch on layout bond paper using a 2B pencil. I then trace the sketch onto Arches 300-pound hot-press watercolor paper and paint the shadow and color using a combination of Dr. Martin's dyes and Winsor & Newton watercolor. The highlights are added with Winsor & Newton designer's gouache. Finally, I use a black Prismacolor pencil to redraw the sketch on top of the colors. This way, the fun of the sketch is preserved in the final illustration.

SIMON & SCHUSTER BOOKS FOR YOUNG READERS
An imprint of Simon & Schuster Children's Publishing Division
1230 Avenue of the Americas, New York, New York 10020

Book design by Virginia Pope
The text for this book is set in Centaur.
Printed in Hong Kong
10 9 8 7 6 5 4 3 2 1

Library of Congress Cataloging-in-Publication Data
Lauber, Patricia.
Around-the-house history: What you never knew about fingers, forks, & chopsticks /
Patricia Lauber ; illustrated by John Manders.
p. cm.
Summary: Describes changes in eating customs throughout the centuries and the origins of table manners.
ISBN 0-689-80479-2
1. Tableware—History—Juvenile literature. 2. Flatware—History—Juvenile literature. 3. Eating customs—History—Juvenile literature. [1. Tableware—History. 2. Flatware—History. 3. Eating customs—History.] I. Manders, John, ill.
GT2948.L39 1999
394.1'2—DC21
97-17041
CIP
AC

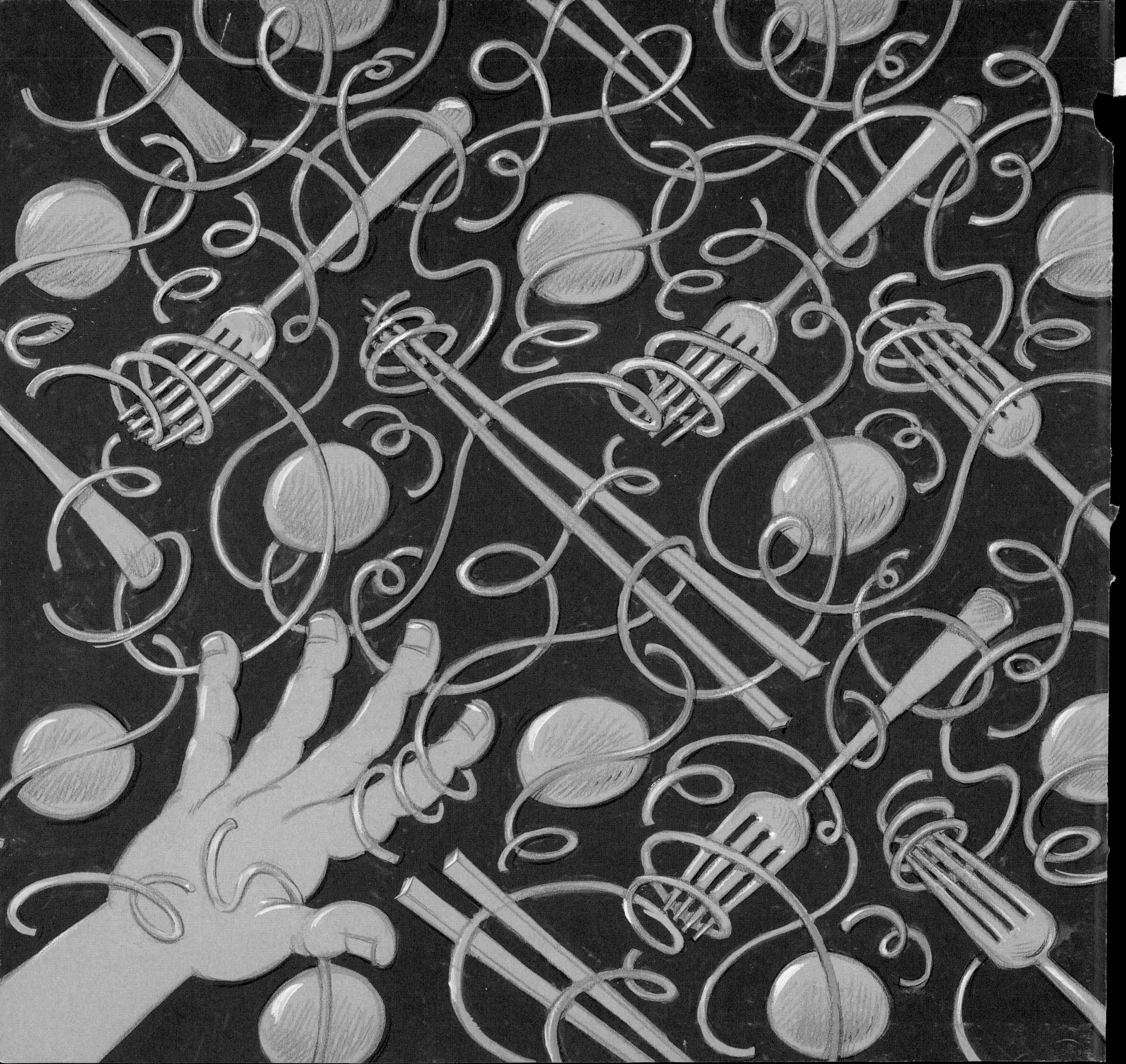